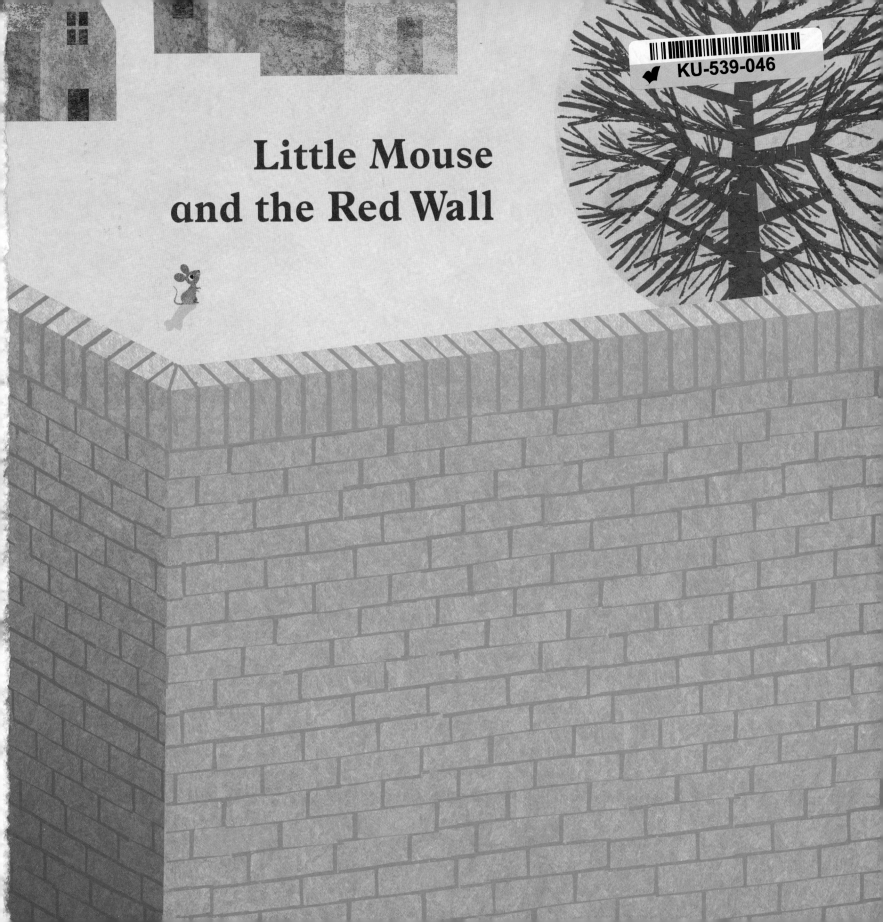

Little Mouse
and the Red Wall

To the fearless –
and a world without walls
B.T.

ORCHARD BOOKS

First published in Great Britain in 2018 by The Watts Publishing Group

1 3 5 7 9 10 8 6 4 2

Text and illustrations © Britta Teckentrup, 2018

The moral rights of the author and illustrator have been asserted.

A CIP catalogue record for this book is available from the British Library.

ISBN HB 978 1 40834 280 0

Printed and bound in China

Orchard Books
An imprint of Hachette Children's Group
Part of The Watts Publishing Group Limited
Carmelite House, 50 Victoria Embankment, London EC4Y 0DZ

An Hachette UK Company
www.hachette.co.uk

Little Mouse
and the Red Wall

BRITTA TECKENTRUP

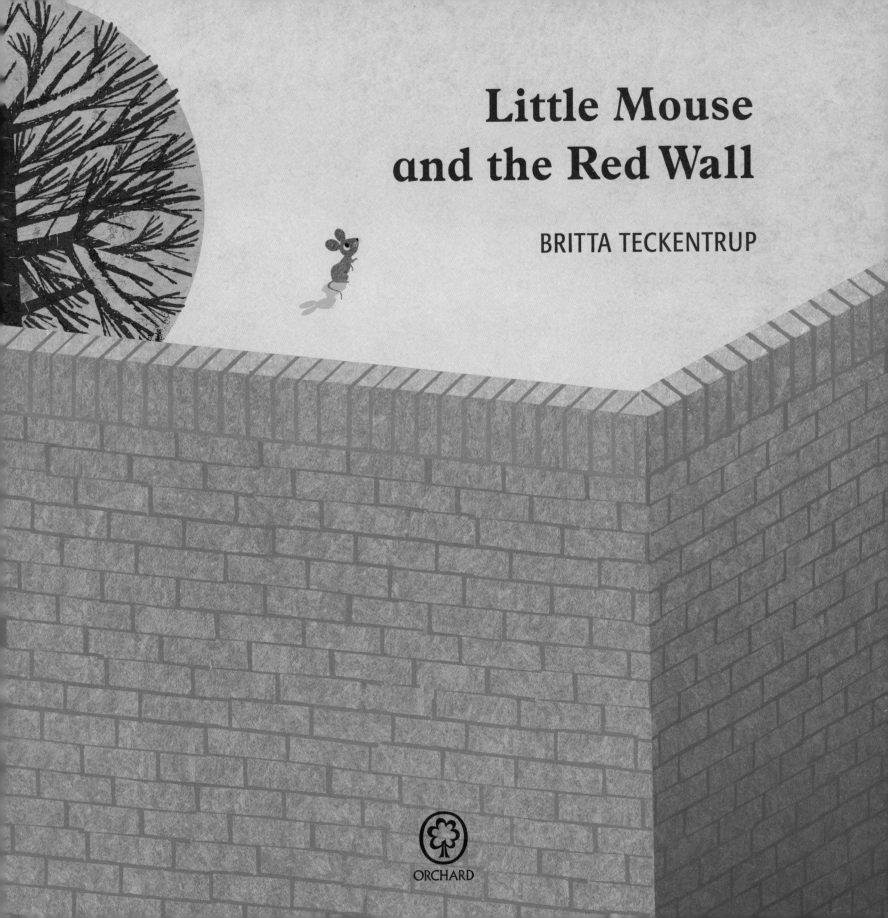

ORCHARD

The Big Red Wall
had always been there.
It stretched as far as the eye could see.

Nobody knew where it began or ended, or how
it had got there in the first place. In fact nobody
seemed to notice it was there.

But Little Mouse was curious. "I wonder

what's behind the Big Red Wall."

Little Mouse asked Scaredy Cat, "Dear Cat,
have you ever wondered why there is a wall?"

"The wall is here so nobody can come in," Cat whispered.
"It protects us, Little Mouse. It's dangerous on the other side."

And she skittered away.

Little Mouse asked Old Bear,

"Old Bear, why was the Red Wall built?"

"I can't remember, Little Mouse," said Old Bear. "The wall has been

here for so long that it has become a part of me, a part of life."

"But don't you ever wonder, Old Bear?" asked Mouse.

"No, Little Mouse. I am too old to wonder about it now."

And he lumbered away.

Little Mouse asked Laughing Fox,
"Do you know what is behind the Big
Red Wall, Fox?"

"I don't care what's behind the wall," grinned Fox.
"You ask too many questions, Little Mouse. Accept
things the way they are and you'll be happy like me!"

And he hurried away.

Little Mouse came across the Lion Who Had Lost His Roar.
"Lion, what is it like behind the Big Red Wall?"

Lion looked sad. "There is nothing behind the wall,
just a big black nothing!" he replied. And he stared
into the distance as if Mouse wasn't there.

But Little Mouse
still wondered.

Then one day a colourful bird flew over the wall.

"Oh!" cried Mouse in wonder. "Where do

you come from, beautiful Bluebird?"

"From the world behind your wall," said the bird.

The other animals stared in disbelief. It couldn't be true!

"Can you take me to your world, Bluebird?" asked Little Mouse.

"I want to find out what's behind the wall."

Together Little Mouse and

Bluebird flew over the wall . . .

. . . and found a land more beautiful and colourful than Little Mouse could ever have imagined.

"I thought it would be dark and scary," said Little Mouse. "My friends told me so."

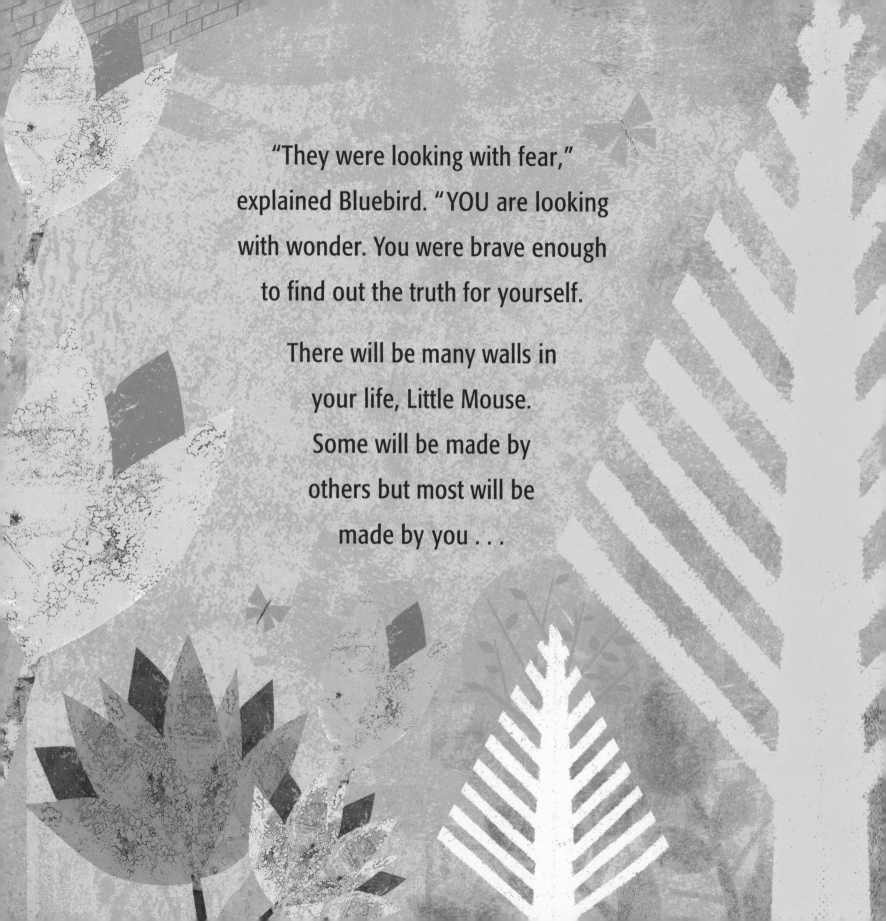

"They were looking with fear,"
explained Bluebird. "YOU are looking
with wonder. You were brave enough
to find out the truth for yourself.

There will be many walls in
your life, Little Mouse.
Some will be made by
others but most will be
made by you . . .

But if you open your mind
and your heart, those walls will
disappear one by one, and
you'll discover how beautiful
the world truly is."

"I have to tell my friends," cried Mouse.

"They may not be ready, Little Mouse," Bluebird warned her.

"I want to try," said Mouse.

But as they turned back, a strange thing happened . . .

"Where is the wall, Bluebird?" asked Little Mouse.

"What wall?" said Bird. "There never was a wall."

And Little Mouse
understood.

So Little Mouse returned to her friends and told them what she had seen. They listened quietly, then one by one they walked through the wall.

Only Lion stayed behind . . .

until the day he too was ready to join
Little Mouse and her friends in the
land beyond the wall.